When a Stand Up Guy Meets a Sold Out Girl

When a Stand Up Guy Meets a Sold Out Girl

Nahtan Hoj

iUniverse, Inc.
New York   Bloomington

When a Stand Up Guy Meets a Sold Out Girl

iUniverse books may be ordered through booksellers or by contacting:

iUniverse
1663 Liberty Drive
Bloomington, IN 47403
www.iuniverse.com
1-800-Authors (1-800-288-4677)

ISBN: 978-1-4401-9987-5 (sc)
ISBN: 978-1-4401-9988-2 (ebk)

Printed in the United States of America

iUniverse rev. date: 12/23/2009

Table of Contents

FOREWORD

Like most stories of this nature, there is always that girl, and that guy, and usually another girl of seemingly less significance and someone (usually the guy) does something stupid, something happens, and feelings get hurt, and somebody has to make it better.

The characters need to be on different planes of existence to create a situation comedy. I feel my character choices are indeed on different planes.

Hopefully my version of a familiar love story is just different enough to be original. So what are you waiting for, start turning the pages.

LONELY DIVA

Suzy Cube is a pop sensation, with chart topping hits worldwide. Her concerts are some of the sexiest shows ever seen, with multiple costume changes and sexy lyrics; she is the epitome of many men's dreams.

It's not easy being popular, the tour schedules and the recording studio take up a lot of her time, and finding a man, any man is, is not something she has much time for. Her entourage hates it when she goes off in disguise to get away from it all, but they know she'll return, because she always has.

None of her incognito trips has ever found her a man, but how many men would believe she was who she said she was anyway? It's not like she can come up to a cute guy and say; "Hey, nice to meet you, I'm really Suzy Cube." Most men would either drool with adoration or run for help. It's not like pop divas talk to the average Joe everyday.

She loves her fried foods, hardly helpful to her girlish figure but wings are her all-time favourite. She is so thankful her tour stop picked Buffalo, so she can go to the Anchor Bar. She only hopes to find a guy she can enjoy them with. All of the Entertainment shows crave to know who she'll be dating and they never find anyone. She's insisted that a celebrity is not the way to go, though they could relate to her lifestyle, they wouldn't be around enough for her companionship.

Suzy stared in the mirror in her tour bus office and spoke.

"Just once I'd like to find a guy right there in the audience, waiting for me. Then I'll know that its fate that brought us together.

It wouldn't hurt if he was kind of cute."

Next stop Buffalo, the stadium was pretty much a sell-out, even if most of the seats were corporate types, schmoozing clients; a full stadium was something she adored performing to.

OPENING ACT

Bruce Meadows is a stand up guy, literally. We find him on stage at a local Buffalo comedy club, opening for a more successful act he's never heard of before. He looks like a young Vladimir Putin, whom is being considered as a sex symbol for the more mature set. His physique is pretty decent for a man of forty, his thin hair is not detracting from his looks in any way, but he's said "no" to several girls mostly because he has an obsession with one famous pop star; that is probably much younger than him. Bruce is the first guy to open a door for someone, and let someone into traffic, provided they do it politely. If they don't drive with courtesy in mind, they become part of his act.

His Thursday night routine begins on stage to crowd of yuppies and generation X types.

"Hey, folks how you all doing tonight?"

A few yells and jeers gave him a feel for the audience, so he starts off his routine.

"Great stuff, who here likes driving to work in the morning?" a quick scan shows that no hands are up. "Fantastic, you hate driving as much as I do."

Some laughs, table slapping, and cheers.

"Have you ever wondered why none of the people you drive behind, can ever signal their ass?"

A heckler yells: "I resemble that remark!"

"Precisely my point pal, maybe if you had a signal to your brain, you could signal a change of a lane. You sure don't drive straight so you must be pissed drunk!"

"Oh, wow a poet in a comedy club." Shouts the heckler.

"At least poets have more intelligence than a loser who can't find a stick on a steering column. Did you even know your lane hopping is increasing your travel distance?"

A few more cheers, putting the heckler in his place.

"Now, have you also noticed, that most motorists… (I use the word motorists, because a driver means someone who is skilled… and a motorist clearly is not) have no idea how to perform simple mathematics."

"They keep driving their rectangular cars into triangular lanes, because they cannot read a diamond shaped road sign!"

"Driving isn't Rocket Science; it's Geometry.

It's a whole lot simpler, unless you're a complete moron."

Loud applause, a few whistles, and a cat call from a girl in the front row.

"Let's consider the rain. Everybody and their brother's uncle's car is some shade of grey. The road is grey, the sky is grey, we can't see your ass that's grey, that's lost in the rain and spray because your lack of grey matter can't find a light bulb today!"

"How about driving in snow? What do you call people that can't clean snow off their cars? The Three Forces Of Evil: Mobile Snowbanks, Defroster Dunces, and the Wipers Only Brigade!"

"How about darkness? Put your bloody lights on, Moron in a Neon! There's this thing called darkness that headlights actually work in!"

"Blocking Intersections, Hell's Kitchen you know the place the light changes and schmucks are blocking your path. If you don't fit, don't be a twit! A side street is not a parking space for assholes, but assholes always park there! Green does not mean go people; it means Proceed if and when the way is clear. If it's not CLEAR it's not WHEN you PROCEED!"

"Stop proving your stupidity, by your inability, to do simple Geometry, and prove to me, your need for a lobotomy!"

"Damn, I got more for ya, but the hook is ready to take me offstage. Thanks for putting up with me."

He takes his cue from the stage manager to let the next act on, and quietly exits the stage.

A few people at the exit door give him some encouragement. "You did good man, there's always one loser ready to mess you up." said one. "Yeah, that tosser was a real dipass." said another. "Hell, yeah mate, love the math stuff, original I say. Lobotomy was a great finish."

Our guy just smiles and starts to open the door to leave, when the stage manager stops him.

"Yo, dude I forgot your name already, we'll have you back for another opener when we got some space. So what's your handle again?"

"Bruce, Meadows" he said.

"Ok, got it Bruce Mellow." And he turned away before Bruce with his hand up tried to correct him.

Now he could leave. After all he had front row seats with backstage passes to the hottest singer on the planet, for tomorrow night. Suzy Cube. Though he was clearly way out of her league, he had high hopes that a meet and greet could allow him to woo her.

He could even use his new stage name; maybe that would work.

Bruce may use some insults in his routine like every other stand up act, but his insults were based in pure logic. He didn't resort to sex jokes, fart jokes, or constant swearing. Logic made more sense. The Geometry vs. Rocket Science angle drove the issue home.

His jobs never seemed to pay all the bills, and every woman that showed an interest in him, he had never felt a spark for. His stage acts had barely paid his very cheap rent and keep food on the table. Between jobs now, stand up comedy was all he had now for income.

He'd pretty much maxed out his Visa credit card for his ticket and backstage pass to Suzy's show. Hopefully it would be worth it. All he really needed was some kind of luck.

THE CONCERT

The concert would start at 8pm. There were a few opening acts that would do about a thirty minute set, of three to four songs, and then the hottest music diva on the planet, Suzy Cube, would take the stage around 10pm and if we were lucky, she would stay until 11:30pm. Her career already entailed five #1 smash hits, so pretty much everything she did went gold or platinum in a week.

From what Bruce could see, Suzy Cube was a short, voluptuous, redhead that wore the tightest medieval bodices you could probably paint onto her, but unlike Lady Gaga, noone had yet questioned her sanity. She looked like a Celtic war goddess, with her hair braided into a massive ponytail or untied in a fabulous red mop. Her music was so popular; she could be like a new Shania Twain or Taylor Swift. Sadly format rules prevented her material on some radio stations, but it never hurt her record sales. That; and the very sexy outfits she changed in and out of constantly on her stage tour.

Bruce was busy going over in his mind how meeting her backstage could potentially change his life. What would he say, how would he introduce himself? What he didn't know is that she was actually looking for someone just like him too.

"Hello, Miss Cube, I am Bruce Meadows, no no that's not it I'm

Bruce Mellow stand up comedian extraordinaire, and I am totally in love with you."

"Hell that will never work; I'll have security detail on me in seconds."

"Miss Cube, may I state that the way you did your hair tonight is divine. I am but a lowly stand up comedian that positively adores your music. Might we spend a moment alone to get acquainted?"

"If that doesn't get me tossed out the door, I don't know what will."

"Miss Suzy, I find you positively radiant and your music is a revelation. May I please give you a tour of our great nation?"

"The poetry angle doesn't work if it's cheesy."

"Hello, Miss Cube, I am your next boyfriend, Bruce Mellow from Buffalo."

"That could work; I think, not too forward, less cheese on the poetry. Bruce you're an idiot, your name isn't Mark Anthony."

He continues to pace, fumbling with keys in his pocket and staring at the mirror from time to time.

"Ok, crap! Ten hours until the concert, stop rehearsing your pick up lines, just meet her and whatever is said is said."

It probably felt like the longest ten hours of Bruce's life, but he persevered to contain his emotions and quietly find his way to his front row seat. No-one was with him; it's not like he could bring a date when his goal was actually to try to date the star. The biggest problem with front row was that he had to crane his neck to see the stage, like at the IMAX cinema.

The first act was an up and coming country band, which was cool, because Bruce loved country music and knew he wouldn't die of boredom for this act. They had a female lead singer and some guys on guitar in the back. Good voice, quite pretty, but when she walked the stage by his seat he could see straight up her miniskirt. Thank god she was wearing something, or he may have fainted. She leaned over the stage to shake hands with the front row, showing her decent cleavage which Bruce got a very good look at.

The second act was a guy trio, more southern rocker type band, anthem type stuff, good times had by all. They could have been ZZTop except they were all as bald as Bruce was.

"Finally!" he checks his watch its 9:25pm

Intermission and time to check out the souvenirs.

Suzy was scheduled to start at 10:00pm sharp.

It seemed like as good a time as any to buy some souvenirs. Maybe he'd grab a cooler, or a beer, though they never sold his beer. The souvenir stands had all the acts, including one shirt that showed all three acts, Suzy on the front, the other two acts on the back, the arena name and some signatures. $45 bucks for that.

Sounds like a good idea, so be bought two. $90 gone. $10 for a cooler, he had about $50 left for the night. Hopefully that covered any food he might possibly be craving afterwards.

Ok ten minutes until she came on stage, time for a bathroom break, and then take his seat for the big show. Something he ate for dinner wasn't sitting too well, so he'd better do the safe option of the toilet stall. After pulling out his stash of disinfectant wipes he took his seat on the toilet. Two minutes to show time and he hadn't even begun to stop doing his business in the bowl. Crap, what did this to him? He was going to miss her opening number, after all the preparation he'd done for this night, he was going to miss her opening number, because of this! Several sheets of toilet paper later, he finally felt he was done, and he exited the stall which had an auto-flush sensor, so he heard it flush as he used the sink to wash his hands. Unfortunately it kept flushing, and the water didn't go down; it went up, and over the bowl. Toilet water hit his shoes.

"Cripes! Holy shit! Dammit...ARRRGGH!"

He ran from the washroom, noone was in it, and the lobby concession area was dead except for employees working the booths and stands. He had to wipe his feet and quietly take his seat in the front row. Suzy was already singing, the song would be over soon, he had to be quick. He wiped his shoes in the tunnel entrance under the upper seats where he found his aisle to the front. There was no garbage can; so he pocketed the wipes in the back pocket of his pants.

"Oooh, not good. Crap! She's almost done the song. Bloody hell!"

He did his best to walk briskly without running or being too noticeable and find his seat, that noone was using, everyone stood in the front bowl area at the moment.

But Suzy's song was her latest hit: Sit Down

Every guy and every girl

Likes to stand around

You can't always do what you want

I told you to...SIT DOWN!

At that moment the entire audience took their cue and Bruce was the only knucklehead standing. As he was getting to his seat she reached for him, grabbing his chin.

I told you to...SIT DOWN!

She pushed him to his chair, and the crowd roared! Still sitting though.

"Just great." Thought Bruce, I'm now the laughing stock of the universe on You-tube tomorrow. Then his front row compatriots started to sneer at him, upturned noses, and the sudden realization that Bruce stunk. No amount of disinfectant wipes or deodorant could mask this stench.

He got up.

I told you to...SIT DOWN!

He sat down. His compatriots got up, and found seats eighteen rows back. There he was alone in one ten person section of the front row, with Suzy Cube singing straight to his face. He thought Heaven wasn't supposed to be this terrifying.

Suzy couldn't believe her luck, this guy just walked into her song and her life, and the people beside him left! He was cute for a bald guy, perhaps a bit older, but his eyes were glued to her. Good sign. She could work with this one.

Then the song ended with Suzy's amazing legs mere feet from his eyes. Her next song was a ballad, where she sat down legs over the stage, and then walked the aisle. Security detail hated these parts. Without anyone directly beside him, he was an obvious target for her performance criteria. She sat next to him and began singing directly to his face.

You're the one I've always wanted
The one I've always needed
It hurts me when you bleed
You're the guy indeed.

And then she stood up, rested her arms on his shoulders, leaned her cleavage to his face, pulled her arms away, lifted her leg over his and trotted back onto the stage with conveniently placed steps that would soon disappear again. Her stage people were brilliant at diverting attention from their presence.

A translucent changing screen was put around her, lights showing her in shadow as she was removing her medieval bodice, which then flew through the air directly into Bruce's lap. He thought he was going to die right then and there. She was beautiful, and had an amazing throwing arm! The lights went off. The screen dropped and she cat walked to the front of the stage wearing not much more than a facecloth sized leather thong over her crotch, and her hair covering her breasts entirely. She turned to show her amazing ass and the miniscule thong thread that passed through it. The lights went out in the arena. Song over, the black garbed stage hands, covered her with a black robe and took her offstage, presumably to find a new costume.

The music began for her third song, which thankfully for her costume changing requirement, had a really long guitar solo. Her music was definitely pop, but the country influence was subtle.

She rose out of a whole in the stage complete with lights from below, wearing what can only be described as a Daisy Duke outfit. High boots, short shorts and a tied top you just want to untie.

Not that it needed much help; it seemed tied so loosely that a slight breeze could open her cleavage to the masses. Her hair was back in pig tails on either side of her head, but probably just long enough to be carefully positioned again.

Though no-one behind Bruce complained of the stench, and the front row area he was in was empty, noone ever re-joined him. It was just bad enough to avoid, yet Suzy had basically ignored that. Was there something there?

Suzy had a head cold, and couldn't smell anything, but figured this poor sod she had been using in the front row must've had some serious stench issues. Hopefully he'd continue as her foil for the night. He looked really cute up close, his eyes never left her.

Another set of stairs appeared and she walked straight back to Bruce. Covering a classic song by Nancy Sinatra and Jessica Simpson. Well, that explained the outfit.

These boots are made for walking
And that's just what they'll do
These boots are made for walking
And they'll walk all over you.

She pulled the zipper off her right boot and pulled it off her leg right in front of his face. Then she put it on his head, she made him unzip the next boot, and pull it off as her arm was busy holding her first boot on his head, while her cleavage sat at his eyes, he had trouble looking at the zipper for the boot, he knew if he pulled the bow off her shirt he'd be arrested in seconds. He handed her the other boot. She had them both on his head, as she pushed her cleavage into his nose. She threw the boots to the audience, and sat in his lap, where she untied the front of her top, moved her pigtails in place, and dropped the shirt to the floor. Lights out again.

Bruce felt his heart racing like mad and started to control his breathing. He didn't know how soon she'd be back, and if he'd be used again as part of her sideshow exploits. Not that he minded being used as her boy toy; after all it was a goal of his to become one. He was pretty sure his pants could not get any tighter between his legs, but he couldn't exactly loosen his belt as the world was watching his every move right now.

Lights were back on, new song, new outfit, with even less imagination. What seemed to be a super tight wetsuit like the Olympic swimmers wear, except that it went around her breasts, and was a thong through her ass again. She had a black lace bra of limited size protecting her innocence, not that she was wanting to.

I want to swim in your love

You fit my body like a glove

It's you I think of

Let me swim into your love

Well, if she suddenly got wet, it could be a disaster for Bruce. She turned towards her band. A curtain dropped on them, she pulled the suit off her shoulders, turned from the audience, and unclipped her bra. Her ponytail was at her back, so it wasn't protecting her frontal exposure. A t-shirt was thrown from the curtain; she reached and caught it, and put it on…white tee, pure white, no writing, no logos, white. She turned towards the audience again walking at Bruce, shoulder straps at her sides, white tee barely covering her ample breasts. Bruce looked up, and saw the massive water bucket suspended above her head. She was going to be wet; her nipples were already erect and barely covered by the tee. Then it fell, she was soaked, the wetsuit at her ankles, her hand between her legs, and all the nipples and skin that could show through a tee. Bruce was wet too; it was a big splash, mostly contained by a large walled mat that suddenly showed up beneath her feet. Carefully strutting with hands between her legs she made him stand and hold his jacket in front of her, while she ripped her tee off, naked as a jailbird right in front of his eyes, but the lights were strobing, so noone except Bruce could be sure she was nude. She put her arms in his jacket and buttoned the front, sliding it halfway over her shoulders to cover her crotch. She gave him a wet kiss and went back on stage. With her back to the audience, she dropped the jacket, and the lights went out!

Bruce was pretty sure he was going to have a serious heart attack if she didn't stop undressing. The net pictures would be rampant; she was practically naked for the entire show so far. How the hell was he going to speak to her calmly after all of this had happened? He still wanted her autograph, part of his whole purpose for having the backstage pass, but so far he'd gotten a lot more than he had expected. He wasn't sure if the people eighteen rows back that used to sit with him were mad, or relieved. Not everyone in the front row had a backstage pass, but he sure hoped that they didn't.

Her next song was another ballad, she came out wearing a very long coat with a large brimmed hat, the coat still showed some leg, but was below her knees.

I have to have you in my life
I need you to have me as your wife
Through hunger and strife
Let me be your wife

Finally, a song she didn't strip to. At last his heart could settle down. He hoped anyway. Alas he was not so lucky. On the final ending bar, she was inches from his face, coaxed him to stand up, get close, and then she flashed her naked body as she burst open her coat. Lights out.

Bruce was beginning to think his crazy infatuation with this sexpot starlet diva was a very big mistake. He'd be dead in a week, if this kept up. It was almost 11:30pm, since she didn't quite have enough material to go much longer without some cover tunes, she'd soon put an end to his boy toy experience.

Final number, on her encore set. She saved her best hit for last, instead of a cover tune which she had filled the time with earlier.

You need me
I want you
I'll let you have me
That's what I'll do
You want me
You take me
That's what you'll do

Final bows, still decent cleavage display, lots of leg, less of the full frontal onslaught he'd been enduring throughout the show. She winked and blew a kiss at him, probably for putting up with her crazy antics. Did she know he would be backstage?

"Wait a minute, my jacket…" She dropped it onstage. "My pass was in it!"

He bugged a security hand, and said that his pass was in his jacket.

"Sorry pal, the stage crew deals with that stuff. I can't help you."

"How can I find it?"

"Look, man, I'll bring you to the stage manager's office, maybe he can help you."

About five minutes later at the manager's office. He motions Bruce to sit down.

"What can I do ya for sonny?"

"My backstage pass was in my jacket, which Suzy used as a prop to hide her body during one of the songs." He paused. "I need that pass."

"Sonny boy, after what she did to you tonight, are you sure your heart can stand much more?"

"Good point, but I have to be there. I need my jacket back."

"I'll radio the band manager, hang on a second." He dials his radio to a different channel. "Hey there, Mr. Suzy Cube manager boy, I got here a fan that was part of the show mostly, as his jacket became a Suzy prop, can ya locate the poor lad's coat for me?"

"Um, yeah, hang on a sec. I'll find him in your office then?"

"That'd be an affirmative yes boy."

"OK, Suzy insisted we let him back, whether he had one or not, and he was gone when we looked for him."

"That's because he asked me for help."

"Got it, ok send him to the backstage door, ask for Brian."

"Got that Lad?"

"I got it. Thanks."

So Bruce went to the door and asked for Brian. When he got there, the doorman didn't know any Brian.

"I was told to ask for Brian, they have my jacket which had my pass. Suzy borrowed…it."

"Oh, yeah, right on mate, ya, the front row guy, lucky dog you are, crud, go right in. Whoever Brian is, he'd probably let you in."

So he sauntered in, hoping to locate Brian who could verify his being there. One of the people that had evacuated the front row gave Bruce another sneer like look and walked away.

A very small man was in front, so Bruce tapped his shoulder for help.

"I'm looking for Brian.."

"You found him, are you the guy I sent here?"

"Yeah, my jacket, was used…"

"Yeah, yeah, Suzy has it, you're good. Go get your autograph and whatnot."

"Um, yeah sure."

So Bruce went to find Suzy Cube's autograph area, but met the first lead singer first.

"Hey sweetie, front row right, never miss a guy checking me out. Down my rack, up my skirt."

"It's not like you gave me much choice."

"True enough, but you're a Cubist aren't you?"

"Oh, you mean a Suzy fan… well yeah, that was the point to getting here, truthfully."

"Look, if she can't see you for the cute guy that you are this is my cell number." She hands him a card and puts it in his pants.

She left him alone, but he had thought she was very attractive.

Then, he saw her; Suzy was in jeans and a tight tee, midriff showing, deep neck, lots of cleavage. He made his way to the autograph line.

A few fans autographs later, and he was face to face with her.

"Hey, hi, sorry for making you part of the show like that, but being all alone I thought you could use the excitement."

"Thanks, I was certainly not expecting half of what I saw."

"Oh the stripping, you mean, you look trustworthy so I felt comfortable getting sexy around you."

"There are probably a million pics on the web by now, you gave very little imagination, none actually."

"Trust me; my lighting guys are the best, only you saw anything that could hurt me."

"Brian said you have my jacket, my pass for here was in it."

"Yeah, no problem, I can give you some more stuff, it's the least I can do, after making you a show highlight."

"Oh, really there's no need for that."

"But first, where do you want my autograph?"

He reached into his back pocket, for a notepad and pen, to find the disinfectant wipe that caused front row people to leave him. He stuttered "Um…yeah…about this."

"I can't smell it; I've had a cold all week."

"So you never.."

"No, couldn't smell a thing, by the way garbage is just over there." She points behind her table for autographs.

He walks to it and drops the wipe in.

"The autograph then, where shall I put it."

"Good question. It seems I'm out of paper, maybe my shirt sleeve…no that's blue…my pants are blue…"

"I got it, come around to this side and sit in my chair."

He obliges her. Not knowing her plan.

She unbuckles his belt and unzips his pants.

"Whoa! Are you planning to…?"

"You're underwear silly; I doubt you'll ever wear this pair again."

"You may be right, especially now."

"Oh dear, a bit wet are we. I'll sign the elastic part at the top." She then re-zipped and re-buckled his pants.

"Look, I'm gonna give you my number, on my card here. We'll talk later OK." She patted him on the back, and then entered her dressing room and shut the door.

"Well, didn't exactly ask her out did I? She asked me? She asked me!"

Now he had phone numbers for two hot women, and an autographed pair of his own undies.

THE PHONE CALL

Bruce Meadows, aka Bruce Mellow according to the comedy club stage manager, had phone numbers for Suzy Cube, and her opening act's lead singer. Both were incredibly beautiful girls that he had never expected a chance with, but Suzy Cube was his ultimate dream. He had to call her.

He had his underwear pinned to his corkboard memo wall in his basement apartment.

"Thanks for the love on stage, Suzy Cube XOXO."

It had dried slightly from his accident during the autograph, but he couldn't wash it. It might ruin the ink.

He stared at the phone for what seemed like hours but may have been only five minutes.

"If I call the other girl…what's her card say…Caitlin, my chances of wooing Suzy are done like dinner. If I call Suzy, and she dumps me, then Caitlin can probably console me."

Sounded like a good plan.

What was the best time of day to call though, it was 9am and the concert ended at midnight or later, he never did check his pocket watch. Surely a pop star needs some beauty sleep, he should wait till noon.

He could wait three hours staring at the phone, or he could get some breakfast and stop worrying about his decision.

The great thing about McDonald's is that they have a great breakfast menu. He ordered a Big Breakfast, extra hash brown, an orange juice and a tea. OK it cost more than an Egg McMuffin, but he just couldn't make himself eat one of those.

That wasted about an hour of his three hour schedule to call up Suzy. He started biting his nails.

"How the hell is she going to go out with me?" he thought. "She's a #1 pop star sold out stadium girl; I'm a back alley comedy club stand up opening act." His mind raced.

After pacing up the streets and back to his apartment, it was now closer to noon. He had to call her. If he didn't call her, his mission was a failure.

11:59 am the phone dominated his vision.

12:00 noon he reached for the receiver, picked it up, and hunted through his pockets for her number.

"No, not Caitlin's number, Suzy's…..ah here it is……555-8347 plus the local area code in front of course."

He dialed….one ring….two rings…three rings….click. He hung up.

On the other end, Suzy just fumbled around her nightstand for her cell, when it stopped ringing. No call display; that sucked.

He stared at the redial button. Seemed like years had passed by, it could have been seconds.

Suzy hoped the phone would ring. She held it in her palm expectantly. Then it did.

"Hello, Miss Suzy Cube speaking, whom do I have the pleasure of speaking to…?"

Bruce was stunned, she answered the phone, he was speechless, which was bad, because she'd hang up. "Um…you're front row guy, man, schmuck, whatever…name's Bruce."

"Oh hi there doll face, I hoped you'd call me, we didn't really get a chance to acquaint properly like."

"No, that would be true in a way; however we made a personal connection I hope last night."

"What, me stripping in front of you, and you creaming your undies during my autograph?"

"OK, but its understandable…isn't it?"

"Look, I'm OK with everything you went through. I didn't give you trauma did I?"

"No, don't be silly, I was only a few beats short of a heart attack every time you came near."

"Ha, ha, funny guy… but seriously, you enjoyed every minute of the attention didn't you?"

"How could I not? The hottest diva on the planet was practically lap dancing for me."

"Well, it wasn't that bad was it? Having a nearly or completely naked singer before your eyes?"

"Well, I think the wetsuit idea was probably an oops on your part."

"Yeah, that was a bit more embarrassing for me. I really thought it would stay on, but the water was too powerful, then I thought I may as well rip the shirt off for ya."

"You didn't have to do that, I mean a million adolescent boys probably have it blown up poster sized in their bedrooms right now."

"I think you'll find that view very hard to find on the web. My lighting guys are amazing, even though you saw me; no camera would have caught me as they all would have had 10,000 Watts pointed straight at them."

"How about I try to Google it then? Suzy Cube strips at Buffalo concert….and 10,000 results displaying 1-10….first one…ok this guy is ticked his camera suddenly failed, he had you plain in his sights, he's so pissed it didn't turn out. Let me try video…that must've been harder to stop.…OK he shows a big white flash with a shadowy figure that is barely discernable…but he describes it as a Suzy Cube private strip tease for the luckiest man in the universe.…I like this guy."

"I told you my crew is the best. Not one bare nipple shot or crotch shot will ever be on the web, butts are fine, and we all can show that."

"Let me Google Suzy Cube wetsuit malfunction… and we have a lot of water splashing shots, nothing really detectable.… video……hmmm it's like your face and body are never visible due to lighting facing the crowds, I thought for sure that would be disastrous for you."

"If you want naked shots of me, you'll have to take them yourself."

"Is this an invitation? I'll have to find myself a camera…"

"You must have a cell phone camera, everyone does, and I do."

"You're completely serious, you want me to take my own shots of you naked for my own personal pleasure, you're not afraid I'll sell them on the web to make a gazillion dollars?"

"You wouldn't do that would you? You seem like such a stand up guy."

"Funny you should say that, because…"

"You do stand up? I love stand up!"

"Yeah, they gave me a stage name…Bruce Mellow…even though its Meadows, do you like it?"

"I love it Mellow-Cube, Cube-Mellow, maybe it doesn't work like a Bennifer does though."

"Maybe Brucezy or Suce?"

"Possibly."

"OK, I'll see when the next gig I open for is, and you can watch me, incognito likely, as noone will expect you to go to a comedy club in a back alley in Buffalo."

"Call me back when you have a time for your show and I'll watch as discreetly as possible."

"You probably have no idea how happy you've made me right now."

"I think it pales to creaming your undies."

"Good point. That would be a different degree of happiness to be sure."

"Remember to call me for the date, we'll sit together for the headliner, or sneak out during their act."

"I will never forget this conversation, expect a call later. Until then you rock Suzy."

"I know Mellow. Toodles."

She hangs up. He hangs up. He dials the club to find out when he's on next.

"Yeah, it's Bruce I opened last Thursday, wondering when I will be on to open another headliner…hopefully soon."

"Oh yeah, Mellow. A few people liked you, wanted you back, next Wednesday good? A week from this Wednesday."

"I guess it will have to, thanks again."

"No probs Mellow, a few more openers and you can get your own headline."

"I hope you're right about that."

They hang up. Now he had twelve days to wait for Suzy to see his show, could he even wait that long?

THE DATE

Bruce redialed Suzy's number to tell her the date of his gig.
"Hi Suzy, its Bruce again."

"Hi hon, when's your show on?"

"A week from Wednesday."

"Wow, twelve days away? Can you wait that long for me?"

I'd much rather see you right this minute to be perfectly blunt."

"Tell ya what, I was planning a day trip to Toronto, see the sights,
CN Tower, Wonderland, and stuff like that. Do you drive?"

"I can drive, I have no car, I don't get paid much, and I live in a
basement."

"No worries sunshine, I'll be at an AVIS rental car place shortly,
incognito of course, it's near the Anchor bar, meet me there for wings
and we'll get the car after."

"Done. I love Anchor bar wings!"

This was going well, Suzy found a guy who loved wings, and he
was cute, and he wanted to be with her. Could it get any better?

They met inside the Anchor bar at 1pm, and planned to enjoy
the famous Buffalo wings of legend.

"You know these are the original Buffalo wings, right?"

"Of course, don't bother with other Buffalo wings, come here and experience the real thing!"

"Um sorry to tell ya, but you have some sauce on your nose." He reaches for a wetnap, then leans over the table to her, and wipes it off.

"Why thank you! Whatever would I do without you?"

"Aren't these the best?"

"Absolutely. Your turn." She grabs another wetnap and leans toward him to wipe his chin. Though her current outfit is lacking a cleavage display, he is still totally in awe of her body.

"So how long have you been singing?"

"Like you don't know? Aren't you my biggest fan?"

"Well, I hope so. Just asking."

"I began with church choir at age ten, a high school band later, and a few karaoke bars, I finally cut a demo CD, and my record label did the rest. How long have you been telling jokes?"

"Stand up isn't really jokes, its monologues, more like poetry mixed with insults and simple logic."

"But for how long?"

"Oh, well, I started writing in my early twenties, tried to sell my stuff to some local headliners, they refused but offered me some opening act slots."

"And you're still an opening act?"

"Well, I travel to different towns, money is tight. If I don't make it in Buffalo I may have to go to Canada."

"There's nothing wrong with Canada."

"I'm not saying that, but the dollar is low there."

"True enough. We are still going there today right?"

"Whatever pleases you?"

After some quick work of a two pound plate, she leaves a tip and they walk out for the rental place. They took a brisk walk to burn off some of the wings protein.

They rent a Mustang convertible, Suzy likes the wind in her hair, she puts him down as the driver, but she pays. A few minutes later they cross at the Peace Bridge into Canada, they answer typical questions, where are you from, see your passports, etc. etc. With no apparent recognition from the customs agent, they head off for Toronto. By 6pm they arrive on the Gardiner expressway, they take a Lakeshore east exit to get to Spadina and find a lot with parking for eight dollars. The CN Tower was a short walk away with plenty of stairs.

"Wow, this place is amazing, you think its tall, but when you're here its just incredible."

"It is an engineering marvel only ever surpassed by the one in Dubai, despite many other claims."

"The whole structure vs. building crap, yeah I know, pathetic designer inferiority complexes, make the competition non-conforming by changing what conforms."

"I think we deserve a trip up don't you?"

"Absolutely, glass floor elevator please."

"No substitutes."

They enter the tower; get their admission to the observation deck and the glass floor elevator.

The elevator attendant has a sixty second speech he's rehearsed for these rides, but Suzy and Bruce are the only ones on this ride, so she decides to react to the ride instead. "Whooooooooooooooooooooooooo oooooooooooooooaaaaaaaaaaaaaaa!!!!!!!!! Awwwwwesssooommme!"

Maybe the guy was finally relieved he didn't have to recite the speech but, her awestruck reaction made him smile.

"We'll let him talk if we come back."

"Sure, of course. Let's go outside."

"Outside???? What do you mean outside?"

"The outside is all bars, no windows, you feel the wind, experience the height, all that."

"NOOOOOOO!"

"Are you scared?"

"Yes. Hold me?"

"I wouldn't think of not doing so."

"This should be against the laws of architecture. You cannot let people this high in the air outside?"

"Think about the guys that built it, I heard Paul Tracy's dad painted it from a harness out of a helicopter. I could be wrong, but I've heard that."

"Paul Tracy, the greatest under appreciated race car driver in Canadian history? That Paul Tracy?"

"The very same. He lived near here; Thrill of West Hill, he could show up at any time perhaps."

And by some miracle he did.

"I couldn't help but overhear you. I'm Paul Tracy. I love Toronto. I hope you do too. My dad did paint parts of the tower outside, but you'd have to ask him how."

"We are some of your biggest fans. Here's an observation pass, can you sign it for me?" pleaded Suzy.

"I'll sign for both of you; do you both have a pass to sign?"

"Yes we do, here's mine."

After that crazy cameo movie moment, they went back inside. The long ride down the elevator seemed less exciting.

"Bruce, how do we get to Wonderland?"

"Its north, I think I can find a way, did the car have GPS?"

"Oh yeah, it did. Duh!"

"Settled then, GPS will help us get there."

About an hour later up Hwy 400 they find the Rutherford Exit to Wonderland.

"Whoa! Is that a Mall?"

"Yup, Vaughan Mills."

"They have a Bass Pro, I love fishing!"

"We can go after Wonderland maybe, if there's time."

"I want to do four coasters, and hit the water park."

"Um do we have any swimwear?"

"We'd better go to Bass Pro!"

"OK, turning right then."

After pulling into a parking space, a few hundred feet away from a main door. Suzy noticed a few other stores. "Tommy Hilfiger! To hell with Bass Pro."

As is usually the case in mall parking lots; idiots park at entrance doors in laneways like they own an emergency vehicle.

It shows a complete disrespect for the safety of everybody else.

"Hey, loser, I'm from Buffalo, stop making my tourist destination a place I want to regret. You don't own a fire truck; get your ass outta here."

"What's it to you dorkwad?"

"I told you what already! Are you just deaf or born stupid? Is English a second language? Are your eyeballs made of manure?"

"Fuck you, dick!"

Suzy decided to speak up. "He's my date, and you had better apologize or I'm calling the cops and having you arrested for assault. My daddy knows all the cops, and he likes to handcuff people."

He started his engine and left, with his finger raised proving his IQ, without the minus sign.

"Thanks, Miss C, but I had it covered."

"No you didn't, you cannot prove stupidity to idiots; they need a fear tactic."

"But, he would have backed down…"

"No, he wouldn't have."

They went to Tommy Hilfiger and found swim suits. Suzy tried hers on and made Bruce come into the change room. "Do you like it?"

"Well, it's less revealing than your stage clothes, so I can live with that."

"I know you love my cleavage, but I need to be incognito remember."

"Yeah, I gotta try mine yet."

"Its ok, we get undressed and dressed together, noone needs to care."

"Its awkward enough seeing yours on here, I don't feel comfortable dropping my pants in front of you yet."

"OK, find another booth and come back."

He does as she says, she calls him in, her suit is on the floor, and her clothes are still hanging.

"Well, I like that honey. Good buns." She quips.

"Nice melons."

"Score!"

"You'd better cover those up. Much as I'd like to stay here all day. I cannot. I don't have a camera for it either."

He leaves heading back to his change room. They both get dressed and head for the cash.

Wonderland is five minutes away by car, so they leave the mall, and head back to the entrance. After paying for parking they walk several hundred feet to the gate. They get through security with her handbag, carrying only her wallet and their bathing suits. He has only his wallet in his pants to worry about. They pass security to get hand stamped for the park. 8pm barely two hours until closing.

"OK, I want to do Behemoth, Tomb Raider, Vortex, and Thunder Run. We'll do the racing slide and Black Hole in the Water Park."

"And then back to the mall?"

"No, dinner silly, somewhere good."

"I saw a Keg. Will that work?"

"For a first date yes."

"Keg it is."

Behemoth was nuts, the lineup was only ten minutes but they thought they were going to die up there, you could see the whole city it was so high. Tomb Raider was not quite as terrifying but you hung to fly like Superman. With the coasters getting less terrifying Bruce had high hopes for the next two.

Vortex was also a hanging coaster but at least you sat in a car type seat, it traveled much of the park after scaring people below the mountain. Thunder Run was essentially the baby coaster, it ran inside the mountain and your sense of direction was removed due to no lights, until the Dragon scared you out of your wits.

"Those were fun, ok now let's get wet."

"Water Park we go then. Time is short and the light is going."

About fifteen minutes of walking and they found the water park area and went to change into their swimsuits. It was still light this late in June. Suzy offered coins for the locker to Bruce. They came out of the change rooms basically together, her Hilfiger suit was strategically holding her breasts and butt from maximum exposure, and Bruce had opted for the long shorts look.

They went for the water race ramp first where you slide on a mat head first down a steep drop with a few bumps to a chequered flag line. Bruce let her go ahead so he could watch her from behind. It was well worth it, even if the suit held her butt in check. They did this three times, her suit getting wetter and less capable of holding her butt in, making Bruce's views better each time.

Next was the Black Hole, a two person inner tube through a dark tunnel to the water below. It had the feeling of a space vortex as tiny pinholes in the tube sent points of light at you while you twisted through the tube, one side was faster than the other. Suzy sat in front of Bruce he held her at the waist, she moved his arms up in the tunnel to her breasts, not that he minded, but it might hurt too much at the bottom, so he dropped his hands right before the setting bright sunlight showed up. The splash was incredible she launched out of his arms as he sank with the inner tube going vertical. When they surfaced the inner tube was behind Bruce, but they faced each other before walking out of the pool. They did four runs with different results at the bottom, he obliged with his hands for her until the bottom each time, his last run she kept his hands stuck on the bra portion of her suit which could have disastrous results if the motions caused his hands to pull the fabric away. So he obliged her insistence hoping it didn't cause her some embarrassment. When they hit the water the fabric did pull as he tried to let go, causing a brief flash to anyone who may have paid attention in the crowd. Suzy did some discreet fixing below water before they left for the last time.

"Did you enjoy that?"

"I didn't realize that might happen." He lied.

"No worries, hon, I enjoyed it!" She didn't.

"OK then."

"I think we've gotten wet enough, let's chill at the wave pool on a deck chair while the sun is still out."

"Well it's getting late. We'd probably dry sooner and get out faster if we just walked. The sun will go down."

"Sure, we could walk, but you wouldn't be able to slather tanning lotion on me while its still here."

"OK, wave pool it is."

After she grabbed her bag from the change room she had her lotion which Bruce methodically spread over her arms and back, and legs, getting close to her butt, while she lay on a deck chair. She turned over, and he began to lotion her legs and arms and stomach, wondering how to lotion her cleavage, he stared at her.

"What's the matter?"

"I can't lotion you there."

"Oh for gods sake why not?"

"This is a public place."

"Just do it. No-one cares."

So he brought his hands towards her breasts, and she pulled him in for a kiss forcing his hands to work their way. His fingers went under the fabric and lotioned around her nipples, then he sat over her body, still kissing, and holding her breasts beneath the fabric. He came up for air, as some spectators pretended not to be looking. He pulled his hands out, exposing her breasts momentarily, just as everyone was turning their heads away.

"I think we need to leave."

"OK, but I totally enjoyed that Bruce."

"We can try it in a less public place."

"Sure."

They went to the change rooms to gather their clothes, but both decided to leave in their suits. A long hand in hand walk to the park gate was having her lean on his shoulder and kiss him spontaneously. He enjoyed the walk. The sun was setting, park lights coming on, the fountain lights changing colour, so they watched from the bridge.

"Bruce, I had a great time."

"I had a fantastic time, can we do this again? I mean spend time together, not here necessarily."

"I hope so, I need a man in my life, and you have been so patient and caring, I don't want to mess things up by not being around."

"Look, you go on tour, I understand that, we can call, Twitter, Facebook, whatever method works."

"Let's just finish the night and see ok."

"OK, but you know it'll crush me to not be able to do this again."

"Let's walk back to the car, its getting cold in this thing."

"Take your top from your bag then, cover up. No need to freeze."

She dons her top and covers her suit, just barely below her hips. They walk out the gate and head for the car. Not a lot of people walking this way, shadows and lights make everything hard to discern.

THE MUGGING

They operate the car remote, and approach the doors, when two men appear.

"Welcome folks, now hand over your money." Says one.

"Yeah, or we do something bad to ya. Or maybe we'll do that anyway."

Bruce pulls Suzy behind him and tries to defend her. "Noone is getting any wallets tonight boys." He hits the panic button.

Beep BEEP Beep BEEP BEEP!!!!

"You sorry little shit, think that's gonna save ya do ya? Well it aint." He punches Bruce in the stomach, and he keels over on his knees. Suzy is no longer protected. He grabs her and pulls her arms behind her back. "See shitty boy, I'm gonna rape your girlie now." His partner helps him hold her down onto the car hood. "Tommy Hilfiger eh? Nice suit you'll never wear again." He pulls the fabric off her butt, and tears it free. "Nice piece of ass honey."

Bruce can only turn his head, as he tries to get up he's winded, and can barely move. The first guy opens his zipper and pulls his penis out. Bruce musters all of his anger and lunges for him. He decks him straight in the jaw. Out like a light, his penis exposed, Bruce stomps on him, and his reflexes make him bend in half. His partner flees. Bruce starts the car.

"Get in!"

"What about him, will you call the police?"

"No way, I'll get assault and you'll get paparazzi all over the airwaves, net, you name it."

"Bruce, we can't just leave him in the parking lot, people will think he was attacked."

"Ok, fine, give me a minute."

He stands over the guy, starting to recover from Bruce's punch; he stares at Bruce whose fist is ready to pound him again.

"No mate, please, I was wrong, I took the wrong path, I'll change I swear."

"Think about it in the trunk." He grabs him and throws him in the trunk; he drives back to the gate. He pulls him out, and takes him to security.

"Hello, this guy and his buddy that fled tried to rape my date, after hitting me in the gut. I got up and decked him, and brought him here, we were at parking D4, and his friend ran north. They tore her bathing suit, I'd show you but she's been through enough. My name if you need it I'll give after you deal with this creep."

"Ok, hang on pal …MIKE! Over here quick. Need some help with a problem."

Mike came over. "Yeah Frank?"

"We need to lock this guy up, he attacked this guy and tried to rape his girl, call the cops to take him away."

"Got it. You're with me loser."

"Thanks Mike. OK Mike will keep him busy. Let me have your details."

"OK I'm from Buffalo I have to return this rental tomorrow morning, I have no hotel booked, my date is not good with identifying herself."

"Name?"

"Bruce Meadows."

"Number you can be reached at?

"I don't have a cell phone."

"Look its your word against his, can she talk? I need more to keep this guy detained."

"OK, but be gentle, she's been through a lot. I don't need her more upset."

"Got it. Miss, sorry to trouble you, can you corroborate this man's statement about the assailant?"

"Certainly, he tried to rape me, his friend held me down on the hood of the car, Bruce hit him hard, he fell, and we brought him here."

"Name? Number?"

She pulls out a card. "Here, I won't always be available, but that's how you can reach me."

"Miss Cube? The Miss Cube?"

"Please don't make a scene. I need privacy."

"Absolutely miss. I'll go see Mike and the suspect…um…detainee."

He left; they never got his full name. Bruce got back in the car and drove out of the park. Vaughan Mills may be open, but it was out of the question. They needed a hotel. The next exit at Hwy 7 was a Hilton, should suffice, and it even had a pool. They parked and Bruce looked for something to cover her backside with as her ass-end was ripped off the suit, and hanging. He found a car blanket stored in the trunk. "Here, wrap this around you like a towel." She got up and did so.

They checked in at the front desk.

"Yes, we have a double occupancy room, one queen size bed, TV, wifi, pool's open till midnight, no lifeguards, please be safe. Are you paying sir?"

"Yes I am." He began, and then she started.

"No, I am. Please, I cannot let you."

"OK, one night or two?"

"One."

"Check out at 11am."

"Great. Thanks."

THE HOTEL ROOM

They went to the room, sixth floor, view of IKEA, last minute deals.

"Look, Suzy, I tried to get up sooner, I wasn't able to move, so winded."

"You did what you could Bruce, he didn't get far, he never touched me beyond ripping my suit."

"I'll sleep on the couch."

"Nonsense. You'll hold me in bed."

"Really, you need space."

"No, I need comfort."

"I feel I let you down."

"No, you saved me. Now hold me."

He held her shoulders and put his hands through her hair, then stroked her arms. She turned and put her arms over his shoulders and reached for a kiss.

"Take it off." She demanded.

"No, I won't." he protested.

"Fine." She flung her suit to her feet.

Her naked body grabbed him by the waist, and then she pulled his swim trunks off.

"Um, lights?" They were all on, window shades up, IKEA had a great view, but it was closed.

She ran for a switch and cut the lights. She jumped onto him; he grabbed her legs in his arms as her arms wrapped his neck.

"I have no protection."

"Screw it. I want you now!"

"It's not right; you're reacting to what happened."

"No, I need you. Make love to me."

He succumbed. His hands crept slowly to the back of her hip finding its way around for a gentle squeeze of her perfect cheek. He picked her up and threw her to the bed. He crawled on top. She rolled him over with her leg. He passionately traced around her breasts with his fingers. She lunged her breasts to his face, he sucked, left then right, then a kiss. She grew impatient and threw herself onto his throbbing erection. Her arms pushed against his shoulders, she rose up and down, he thrust his pelvis with her, and they rolled back and forth. He sucked her nipples again. She screamed in ecstasy. He felt a burning, he was about to explode, she rode him up and down, breasts in his face. Climax. In unison. They sighed together and she fell limp on his chest, remaining on top.

A few minutes later they tried to disengage. "Where's the Kleenex?"

"Bedside table, full box in plastic still."

She ripped open the plastic and started to wipe her body clean. He grabbed a few and did the same. She turned the light on again, and held his arm. "Thank you!"

"You're amazing." He replied.

She smiled and crawled into the covers. He went to the bathroom first. Then he crawled in after her.

She turned to him and said "We'd be better off with me behind you, at least to be able to sleep."

"Yeah, sorry, this experience is beyond words for me,"

They exchanged positions. It felt good to be in her arms.

The sun rose, and woke them at 7am. Four hours until checkout. A few more romps and Kleenex and then they could put their clothes back on.

"Thanks Bruce. I'll never forget this."

"I will never forget it either."

He watches her walk to the bathroom and shut the door. He looks for his clothes, and starts to get dressed. She returns as naked as she was when she left, grabs the clothing bag and goes back to the washroom.

She didn't entirely close the door, so he tried not to watch, but was drawn to her beauty. He adjusted his belt and put on his shoes. He walked closer to the door, as she opened it.

"Were you peeking?"

"Um, no, yes, sorry, tried not to."

"It's why I left the door open silly."

"Um, sure, ok, no harm done."

She grabbed him for a long passionate kiss. She grabbed for the room key, and left him wanting.

They quickly scanned for anything they might leave behind, and decided they had everything they brought with them. They walked out of the room, and she locked the door.

THE FIGHT

They hopped in the car after checking out of the hotel, for the long ride back to Buffalo. Barely a word was said, just smiles and flirty eyes. Was it a one night stand? Would she send him on his way? He wondered. She seemed so genuinely attracted to him, and they did have unprotected sex, he stopped her attackers, and they had a wonderful time.

"Suzy…?"

"Bruce…?"

"Will we see each other again? Was I just a fling for you? Or do you really have a thing for me?"

"I can't believe you, you think last night was a fling?!"

"No, I enjoyed every minute. Did you?"

"Of course I did! Can't you tell?"

"I'm sorry, no I can't."

"You think I'm using you. You can't feel anything? We made love last night."

"Yes, and it was wonderful, but I'm not convinced it was real, any woman can do a Meg Ryan impression."

She punches him, which makes him correct his steering as they are on a highway at speed.

"I want to say I love you, because I do, I just can't believe you feel the same."

"Because I didn't say it? The sex wasn't enough of a clue for you."

"Well, yes."

"Bruce, for fuck sakes, I love you!"

"I love you too. I've never had sex that good in my life, I want more."

"So, I'm your sex slave now? You love me for the sex? Is that what it's about?"

"No, that's great, but I've been in love with you as a pop star long before we met, the culmination of my personal concert experience, this date, the sex, all of it, has solidified my feelings."

"So you love the pop diva. What about the girl sitting next to you?"

"I love the girl too."

"I don't hear it in your voice."

"Honest, you could be Abigail Smith for all I care, I love you, Suzy Cube or not."

"Who's Abigail Smith?"

"A name from thin air."

"No, she was a school fling wasn't she?"

"OK, grade seven, she had a class party at her place, they played Stairway to Heaven non-stop."

"That sounds annoying."

"I didn't care, I stared at her all night, danced with her once, and got chewed out about being out of her league by Dave Williams."

"What's worse, Dave is now dating my next crush from high school."

"Her name?"

"Nancy Henderson."

"Do you Facebook these people?"

"Nancy, she plays scrabble type games."

"You still have feelings for her?"

"Well, yeah, but it's been over twenty years."

"How old are you?"

"Thirty...nine."

"Yeah, right."

"You're what twenty five?"

"You'd be surprised. I'm much older."

"You don't look it."

"It's because I'm a vampire."

He braked and pulled off to the shoulder of the highway. "Please tell me you're joking."

"What? That I'm a 2000 year old vampire. A Celtic Legend named Scatach, a warrior maid. Look it up on Wiki."

"You're messing with me."

"Well, yes, but its how I took my name, Suzy Cube is from first two letters of Scatach."

"So you just modeled yourself on her. The leather bodice is to look like her right?"

"Exactly, though I doubt women showed that kind of cleavage in those times."

"We might be here a while. Traffic is heavy but fast, and gas is low."

"How low?"

"Empty."

"How empty?" Then the engine shut off.

"Real empty. A vampire maid huh? I should have remembered that book."

"Nicholas Flamel, great series. She was a vegetarian, not a blood sucker."

"How are we supposed to get home?"

"I'll call someone on my iPhone."

"I'm sorry about the gas."

"Fine. My manager can send a truck across the border. I'll check the GPS in my phone."

"So are we mad or not?"

"Well, I'm not thrilled that I'm still like a dream to you."

"How could you not be? I'm an average Joe, noone knows me, and you're Suzy Cube the hottest biggest selling pop diva on the planet."

"You can't get past that?"

"The vampire thing helped a bit."

"So you could date a 2000 year old vampire?"

"Yeah, that would be surreal."

"Should I bear my fangs?"

"I don't see them."

"Be serious now."

"How? You wanted me to see your fangs."

"OK, good point."

"So how old are you really."

"Thir...twenty nine."

"Ok so 40 and 30 huh?"

"We have trouble with the zeros. At least we have that in common."

"Let me call my manager."

She walks around the car, telling her manager what happened and where the GPS says they are. After complaining about her incognito disappearance, he gave her a two hour window.

"OK, so we're stuck here, for about three hours or more."

"No, the vulture trucks will arrive shortly."

"Just tell them we have auto club."

"What if he works for one?"

"The other auto club."

"Um, yeah, of course."

A tow truck arrives, and tries to get some business. Naturally he has an auto club logo for CAA.

"Hello, yeah, we're good; our club is coming to tow us. Thanks anyway."

"What club? CAA is the only club in these parts."

"Well, we're American, AAA is coming."

"They cannot cross the border."

"Well, you can't either."

"Look, I cannot allow another vehicle to tow you. Put the vehicle in neutral."

"Maybe, you don't understand. We don't need you."

Suzy came over, smiled and opened her wallet. "How much to go away?"

"I cannot be bribed ma'am."

"Ma'am? I am not a ma'am!" She hits him with her bag.

"OK, I'll leave, but before your guy arrives, there will be plenty of my compatriots."

"CB them to ignore us."

"Fine. Suit yourself."

He pulls away. Suzy's truck comes about two hours later. It's a bigger tow truck with more passenger room.

"Hi Suzy, your manager gave me your GPS coordinates."

"Fine. Just get us back to Buffalo to return this thing."

Though the ride gave them enough room to sit comfortably, they squeezed together.

"I don't have a screen for you guys."

"It's ok, we just had a small fight, trying to heal some of that."

"OK, but your manager isn't paying. You need to decide."

"I'm paying this one; I ran it out of gas."

"Don't be ridiculous it's too expensive."

"I have a Visa, I'll charge it."

"Can you pay it off?"

"Not right away, I have sporadic work. In fact I only have free time because I have no work."

"So I'm supposed to let you, Mr. Unemployed, pay for this tow truck. Be serious now."

"I'll find more gigs. It won't take that long, my rent is cheap."

"I won't let you."

"Because I'm poor? Because you're filthy rich? Thanks, I'm such a low life to you."

"Well, you sound like one now."

The tow truck driver pulls over. "Guys, I don't want to upset your lover's quarrel, but the way I see it pal, stop being the man, she's paying, let her, best way to keep her around. If you ain't got it anyway, why make yourself more broke than you need to be?" He exchanges glances, they nod, and he drives back onto the highway.

"Fine, pay for me, I'll pay you back, I have to pay for something, you can't tow me around everywhere…no pun intended."

The driver chuckles.

"Look, Bruce, you keep on about this and we'll have to part ways. I can't have this tension."

"Ok, so we don't agree once, and that's it. Sayonara Brucey? Nice knowing ya, thanks for the good time, I'm off to find another lackey?"

"If you put it like that…YES!"

"FINE!"

"FINE!"

"How far to Buffalo? I need some separation."

"An hour at worst, depends on customs, lights, the agency deciding if they want to charge you more, yadda yadda…"

"OK, I get it. Just tell me when we arrive."

Customs didn't seem to care about a car towed across the border, that didn't delay them much, the rental agency wasn't happy, but decided for unknown reasons to give them the benefit of the doubt. They parted ways, she paid the bill, and he started walking. She looked for him, but he was gone.

GETTING DRUNK WITH THE OTHER WOMAN

When Bruce got back to his apartment, he looked for stuff to throw. Pillows, books, lamps, anything large and throw worthy. When the lamp shattered into a million glass fragments that cut his toes, he stopped. He limped to his washroom for band aids. When he got back to his couch, he realized he had to clean it up. He dust panned it and tossed it in the trash. He crashed on the couch, and then he saw the card, the other girl Caitlin. He called her up.

"Hiya, is this Caitlin?"

"Yes, who may I be speaking?"

"Bruce, we met, front row, backstage, you liked me checking you out."

"Oh, the rack gazer. Yeah, are you free later tonight?"

"I am, I need a good long nap first, and where should we go? I mean what should we do?"

"Look, hon, I just want to get drunk somewhere, maybe you can get lucky after too."

"Sounds like a good plan. Suggestions?"

"Ok, my band mates like this Irish pub in town, O'Grady's I think."

"Yup, know it. I'll see you when?"

"8pm Sharp baby."

"Ok, so 8:45 pm it is."

"Funny man eh?"

"Yes, actually, what day is it?"

"Sunday morning. 8pm is in ten hours, by the way. Set your alarm and whatnot."

"Yeah, whatnot got it."

They hung up together.

She arrived at the pub by 8:30pm, early considering a girl should be fashionably late. Bruce came at 8:45pm on the dot.

"Hi Bruce is it?"

"Yeah, Caitlin right?"

"Yes, sir. Now buy me a beer."

"Certainly."

They take seats at the bar; they take the pint of the best Irish beer on draft each, Caffrey's.

"I guess Guinness only comes in cans here."

"So I'm told. This is good though, Irish is good beer you know."

"Do you wanna get drunk laddie?"

"Aye, lassie I do."

"Maybe we need something stronger?"

"Like some whisky?"

"Drambuie!"

"Liquid fire!"

"Exactly!"

"OK, I can take it."

"Barkeep, a few shots of the Dram for me lad here, he needs to get drunk fast."

"Is he driving?"

"Hell, I can't afford the bus."

After he downs the shots, his vision is quite impaired; Caitlin looks like a three headed monster with six breasts. He reached to touch them, but misses.

"Ok laddie, you want some lassie time I see. Let's pay the tab and be off then."

He hands her his wallet, she shoves it back down his pants, and pays herself.

"Dammit woman, do I look that broke?"

"Aye you do look it."

They hop in a cab, she directs the driver to her hotel, the tour with Suzy gave them good rooms in the next best hotel, but as long as she stayed, they stayed. As he arrived she handed him some bills.

"Keep the change boy."

He drove off. Caitlin carried Bruce with his arm over her shoulder. The doorman offered to assist her with him to the elevator.

"Much obliged."

Once the elevator stopped, she dragged him to her room. She tossed him on the bed and then went to the bathroom. He groggily got up, realizing his whereabouts had changed.

"Where the fuck am I?"

"You're about to fuck me in my hotel room. Is that all right?"

"Sure, you have like eight breasts; you must have like four vaginas."

"Yup, you're wasted, makes for good sex though, pity you may not remember."

She unbuckles his belt, unzips his pants, and throws her hands into his underwear. His manhood hardens immediately, and she pulls it out. She then rips open her top, braless, jugs waving like leaves in a breeze.

"Wow, how many nipples is that?"

"Just find one, and start sucking boy."

He tries to suck, and misses, getting her shoulder. He tries again, gets her stomach.

"A little higher this time."

He finally finds one, and hangs on, sucking hard and long, using his hands to caress the opposite breast. But as drunk as he was his sucking moved to her elbow.

She put him flat on the bed. She threw her other breast to his mouth, and then pulled her skirt and panties off. Legs over his waist, she grabbed his cock to engage her vagina. Success.

"Ok laddie, keep sucking, I'll do the work down below." She rose up and down quickly and slowly, driving him to ecstatic bliss.

"You are amazing. Why do you have four heads? Whoa, where'd all that skin come from? Hey my dick is gone!"

She threw his head back down, and put her breast back in his mouth as she continued her lunges, he lunged back.

They climaxed a few seconds apart, her first.

She rolls, off and cleans up. She leaves him wet and dirty on the bed. The phone rings.

"This is Suzy's manager calling to inform you of the next tour city, Toronto Canada. Suzy would like to say a word or two…hang on."

"Suzy here, is this Caitlin?"

"Yes, it is she."

Bruce moans.

"Did I hear someone? Are you busy?"

"Nobody, just a guy."

"Hey, I hear someone." Bruce yells.

"Wait a minute, I know that voice."

"Don't know how Miss Cube, he's just a fan, you met him and all, but know his voice I doubt very much that's possible."

"Bruce is in your room."

"Um, yeah, I think the name is the same."

"No, that's my Bruce. The insolent bastard."

"Miss Cube, it's all my doing he's too drunk to know what's happened."

"Hey, is that Suzy? Are you talking to Suzy?"

"Now look here Mr., the lady Suzy thinks she knows ya good, so does she?"

"Yeah, we spent the night, last night."

"Thundering tarnations, he's using me to rebound? He called me because you ditched him?"

"We split from each other. It was about money mostly, and his not being rich."

"Well, he cannot possibly have your money; you're a worldwide super pop diva for fucks sake."

"I know, and he resented that."

"Let me hit him for ya."

"No need. You can have him. I can't be with a man who goes for another woman as soon as he parts the other."

"I don't want him Miss Cube; he's just an easy night of sex. There is no relationship."

"Well, make one, and the bus leaves at 9am sharp, hotel has the info, checkout won't be a problem. You're still on the tour, I'm not vindictive."

"Fine by me, the band will know shortly."

They hang up. She looks at Bruce, prone on the bed, moaning like he was sick.

"OK laddie, so I'm your castoff. You have a romp with Suzy, she tries to buy something, you resent being poor, so you call me, do I have this right?"

"Um…yeah…pretty much. Kleenex?

"Soil your undies for all I care. I'm only good enough for second, I wasn't first?"

"OK, I was wrong to rebound, but we mutually hate each other now, I needed to get that drunk."

"I'm only letting you off, because you're so fucking cute. Let me find the Kleenex."

She cleans him off, and they get dressed. She sends him home.

THE REVELATION

When Bruce got back to his apartment, his senses started to kick in.

"Suzy was mad at …what was her name…Kate? No…Caitlin… yeah mad at her, for being with….me."

He pondered the thought.

"She's in love with me. Suzy Cube loves me. I love Suzy Cube. I'm the biggest idiot on the planet!"

Then he remembered.

"Holy crap. The tour leaves, tomorrow morning, how the hell can I stop her to tell her?"

His mind races, he paces, he becomes exhausted and falls to the floor, where he sleeps.

He wakes up several hours later. He looks at the time. 8:45am.

"Jesus, they leave at 9am!"

He goes to the bathroom, and then hunts for clean clothes to wear. Then he decides better of it, and runs out of his apartment forgetting to lock the door.

THE TOUR LEAVES

8:55am and he's a few blocks from the hotels. 9am they leave, they'll be on it by now, both women, they might both think he's looking for them, but one he isn't.

"Shit, 8:57am still a block away, the engines have started by now."

He rounds a corner, sees the bus, and it starts rolling, towards him. He can wave at the window…but which window, the glass is tinted, he can't see in!

"SUZY! I LOVE YOU!"

There, he said it, was she on the bus? Did she see him at all?

Caitlin was on the bus, Suzy was elsewhere.

She saw and heard what Bruce said. She had to decide if she'd tell her. He wasn't a bad guy, but he wanted the other woman. Would she get over her jealousy to help them?

Bruce ran after the bus for a whole block, losing breath, and sweating bullets. He hoped she saw him, but if she did, she was gone. Back to Toronto where they were the night before last.

No wonder she didn't wait for his gig, she wouldn't even be in town.

Suzy was in a car with her manager, it was safer than the bus, and she actually left much later. She didn't look out the window to see Bruce, nor did she hear him. Her head scarf and large sunglasses kept her disguised from hotel guests while she made her way to her manager's car in an underground lot.

Her manager spoke. "Suzy, everything all right? Did that guy hurt you?"

"Not physically, just emotionally."

"That's always worse, harder to heal."

"I don't know if it can."

"Was he nice at least?"

"Perfect gentlemen. He even protected me from an attacker."

"You didn't tell me this."

"You didn't ask."

"Why did you fall out?"

"He's not rich like me, and felt disgraced that I would insist on paying for everything."

"And he left?"

"Yeah, found our opening act and screwed her too."

"Oh dear, so you had sex with him."

"He had just saved me."

"Understood. What happened to the attacker?"

"The park security was holding him for the cops, I left my number, they haven't called."

Just then her cell phone rang.

"Suzy speaking."

"Um, Miss, Officer Spezza York Regional police, we have your partner, and your statements, he didn't leave any contact number. This is regarding the attempted rape suspect."

"That's right, because he's never home, I'm not sure if I have it saved on my phone, I can't check while we talk."

"Miss, it doesn't matter, the suspect confessed to doing it, he's locked away in holding, and we just need to send you court documents to appear as a witness/victim regarding his partner that fled."

"You'll have to go through my public relations guy in Los Angeles, I'm on tour now, and actually I'm headed that way to Toronto. Can you send an Officer to Rogers Centre? The events manager will know how to find me, and I'll give you the details there."

"I have man willing to go out of his way for that, provided you autograph something for him."

"Fair enough. I don't need press on this situation. It's bad enough having happened, I don't need to world to know about it."

"Miss, I wish I could say we could stop that, but it's made the local paper. Not the National ones from Toronto, but our Vaughan Citizen. It's largely ignored as most of the stories are about councilors and money matters. You were printed on page twelve. Real small piece."

"How long before Toronto papers see it?"

"Could be printed today, I haven't looked."

"Thanks for your honesty."

"I'll wait for my man to find you later today. Then I hope your tour goes well."

"Thank you officer. Goodbye."

They hang up. She stares at her manager.

"So we may have a problem?"

"Depends on if the national papers found the story; and whether it's printed."

When they arrived in Toronto they hunted for the newspaper boxes. Sun, Star, Post, Globe all with headlines:

SUZY CUBE BACK IN TORONTO AFTER BEING RAPED IN WONDERLAND

They had used a generic concert shot from the Buffalo concert, a fully clothed version. It did portray her as flaunting her body.

The Sun, had her as Page 3 girl, a shot of her leather thong outfit and bare back with her head turned. It was highlighted in small frame on cover page.

"So much for a lack of publicity."

"Reporters are probably going to want my statement before the show."

"No, no access to them, just cover the show, no interviews, you need more privacy."

"Ok, just get me to the Rogers Centre."

"Girl, it'll always be Skydome to me, home of the Jays 1992 and 1993 World Series Champs."

"Whatever. Just get me there."

Within ten minutes they found their secret entrance underground, and traveled through the underground parking for their reserved spot.

The York Region officer was there.

"Hello Miss."

"You need my info right?"

"Yes and an autograph if it's no trouble."

"None at all, where would you like it?"

"I brought my pad, and pen."

"Ok, here's the info you need." She hands him a slip of paper with address and numbers.

"And I'll sign that pad of yours."

"Thank you Miss."

"Do you have tickets?"

"No Miss."

"Give me a minute." She enters the events manager office, and

GO AFTER HER

Back in Buffalo, Bruce realized he had to get back to Toronto, preferably with tickets to her show. His Visa was already in trouble for her last concert tickets, front row and backstage was a monstrous price. He'd take nosebleeds. He found Ticketmaster and searched for tickets, there were a few nosebleeds left, only $40 Canadian. He clicked them for his basket, input his Visa, and printed his tickets. Now he had to get there. It was noon, show at 8pm, meaning she'd be on around 10pm again.

Ten hours, rental car, or bus, better take the bus.

"Ok, tickets, bus schedule, find something to give her when I get there, like roses."

He headed for the bus terminal.

Bruce arrived in Toronto near the Train Station which was several blocks from the Rogers Centre, but it was only 5pm. He had time to spare.

As he walked by Union Station, where several vendors had roses; he ran over and bought a bundle. $25, they didn't have means of currency exchange, so they gave it to him for $20 US.

A few more blocks to the Rogers Centre. He passed the

Convention Centre and found Baton Rouge restaurant, prices were steep. He hunted for something cheaper. He found a Tim Horton's

A few donuts would have to do for dinner.

6pm now, people were already lined up at the gates. His was at Gate 13. After he walked to the gate area, the doors opened, and the lines began to move.

As he got inside and had his ticket scanned, the ticket checker insisted that the roses had to stay.

"You're not allowed to bring items that can be thrown."

"Ok but I can buy drinks, which are throwable right?"

"Are you suggesting that intention?"

"NO! I just think the rule is insane, I paid good money for those and need them for later on in the show."

"I will hold them for you. Come back to this entrance and you can have them back."

"That will have to do."

He finds his way to the ramps and finds out just how high his seats are. 500 level.

The curtain blocking the seats which cannot see the stage was directly beside his seat, the roof was directly behind his head. Closer to 7pm now, time to find souvenirs and a drink.

Most of the concessions were under renovation on this level by some company with a giant U logo in green. He had to travel the ramps down to lower levels for food or drink.

"Pizza! Thank god. Holy crap $8 a slice!"

After wolfing down four slices of Pepperoni, he finally felt like he had dinner.

They only sold Labatt and Smirnoff Ice for drinks; he'd have to settle for Smirnoff. They poured it in flimsy plastic cups and it practically overflowed before they handed it to him. Cheaper than pizza barely.

How was he going to enjoy a show from the rafters, when the last one was like a private show from front row? He'd have to see. Back up the ramps to find his seat again. 7:55pm already.

The concert began as he found his seat. It was literally the worst seat in the house. Noone was near him, the fans went on a forty five degree angle from the lowest row to the highest, except for his. The curtain was very close; he decided to slide over a few seats for a better view. Caitlin looked great from up here; she had a good response just like Buffalo.

"If I just peek behind that curtain, could I see her?" He thought.

He decided to look behind, clear view of backstage, he would see everything. He thought he should stay; no ushers or guards bugged him. He went down to front row of 500 level.

After finding a seat at the front of level 500, he looked down to see if lower seats were possible. The other curtains used to shield the stage area were too high to see over from 200 level. Caitlin would be finishing her set. He needed to make her notice him, so they could talk. Her number finished and she walked backstage. He stood on the seats he found, and yelled down to her. "Caitlin!"

She paused, looked up and waved.

"Can you do me a favour?"

"You're here for her aren't ya?"

"Yes, sorry, I am."

"No worries laddie, what do ya need?"

"I need to get backstage before she goes on. This area was all I could afford, and I snuck behind the backdrops."

"I'll find ya."

"No, meet me at Gate 13; I need to pick something up."

"OK, see ya soon."

He checked for security before exiting his seating area, and made his way back to Gate 13.

"Hello laddie, now what's this thing you're needing?"

"I have to ask the ticket taker for my roses back. She said she'd hold them for me."

"Ok and I can help ya retrieve them."

"That I hope."

They soon find the woman looking after his roses. "Oh, here so early? These can be had after the show."

"Well, it's vitally important I have them before 10pm, and I get backstage."

"I can't get you there, nor can I allow it."

"Aye, ma'am but I can, and I aim to."

"And you are?"

"The opening act silly!"

"Oh, bless me, sorry for my presumptions."

"No bother. You just hand him his roses back, and I'll worry about his other task."

She heads for a storage cabinet and grabs the roses, and hands them back.

"Might I ask why and for whom?"

"This perfect gentleman is courting our headliner Miss Suzy; he rode a bus from Buffalo to find her."

"He's that guy? The front row guy she was very personal with, they're an item?"

"Yes and a little bit no. He's trying to win her back."

"But it was three nights ago! You lost her in two days?"

"I was stupid. To be fair we dated the day after."

"Damn straight you were stupid."

"I was jealous."

"I'll give you that one."

"I rebounded with her." He looks at Caitlin.

"You witch!"

"I dinna know that then ma'am!"

"OK, I forgive you. But you sonny child, you are damn well gonna apologize to Miss Suzy!"

"Um, the roses are part of that, I'm just saying."

"OK, now honey child you get him there pronto, I'll have to blame you for everything, you understand?"

"Perfectly. Ok Brucey, let's find your girl."

They make their way through the corridors below, to end up backstage. The second act was still performing, they'd be off soon. Suzy would enter the backstage area from the stage right just before 10pm. He had to be there, with the roses, to tell her, what he came to say.

The band finished their set, and walked through where he stood. She'd be here in less than twenty minutes. Caitlin hid behind curtains with a thumbs up sign, encouraging him.

Even though it seemed time was racing, it suddenly slowed to a snail's pace. She had arrived, her amazing red hair glowing like she was an angel. She spotted him, and stopped.

"Suzy, I messed up, I was wrong, I know that, I should have listened to you, I shouldn't have been stubborn, and I never should have seen Caitlin. I got drunk, I was stupid, and I had to see you."

"Go on. Is there more?"

"Yes, yes there is."

"And?"

"I love you."

"Can you hold on a minute? I have an entrance to make."

"Um…sure…"

She heads out to the stage, and starts talking to the crowd. "Hello, Toronto!"

The crowd goes wild; they settle down and allow her to speak a bit more. "I love Toronto, I was in the CN tower the other day, there should be a law against no windows that high up in the sky."

The crowd laughed with her.

"I had the best time there, with a guy."

Half the audience gave a huge sigh, as though they had a chance to be with her.

"I sort of met him at my last concert, he thought we'd be all over the web, me naked, and him with me, but my lighting guys are so damn good, none of the pervs cameras showed anything."

A loud fan in the front yells. "But he saw everything didn't he?"

"Damn straight he did, and more later."

"Man that guy is lucky." He responded.

"Not half as lucky as I am. See that guy is here, that guy saved my life, when I went to Wonderland with him the other day, some thugs tried to rape me, don't worry they didn't get far. My guy, decked the one trying to get lucky with me, stepped on his nuts and stuffed him in our rental car's trunk, handed him to security, and made me feel safe."

"Is he here or not?" yelled another fan.

"Thanks for asking. How about I let him tell you? Bruce, get your butt out here."

He pokes his head out of the curtains, he can't see a thing, because of the lights, and he slowly makes his way to her on stage and stands next to her.

"Come on Bruce; tell them what you told me backstage."

"I can't say all that to all of them."

"Not all of it, just the last part."

"I love you."

"They can't hear you, don't you guys want to hear him, and don't you want him to say it so we can all hear it?"

The crowd roars approval.

He takes the mike; he kneels in front of her.

"Suzy Cube, I love you!"

The crowd cheers.

She gives him a bear hug and kisses him long and passionately on stage.

"OK, Toronto, thanks for letting me have that moment, now let's get ready to PARTY!"

Her concert goes much like the one in Buffalo, the songs were rearranged slightly and the costumes were the same, just without the lonely boy toy in the front row to work off of.

As the concert ended, on her last encore, she shouted to the crowd. "I love you Toronto!"

They all cheered and she came backstage, Bruce still had the roses, she pulled him back out.

"And I love my guy! Thank you!"

They left the stage. She took him to her dressing room, where they had passionate sex. The backstage party would begin shortly, she would meet the cop there, the one that she had given passes to.

Once at the party she noticed the officer, and asked him if there was more news.

"Yes, Miss, the other guy, the first guy gave us his name, his address, his phone number, the whole deal, he had to confess to. Since they both confessed though, there won't be a trial. They are under lock and key."

"Thank you officer, I hope you enjoyed the show, and this party."

"Yes, miss I did, and I am."

After she did all of her autographs for everyone, she found Bruce. "What's say you and I go on a road trip…."

"Let's find a different rental agency."

"LOL!"

"Avis isn't likely to give us a car that we forgot to fill it up."

"OK what agencies are there here?"

"Budget I think. I have a Sears Card."

"Oh, for crying out loud, I'm paying!"

"Let me think about that….ok dear."

"We have to wait a few hours yet."

"Gee I wonder what we could do in your hotel room? Isn't it in the stadium?"

"As a matter of fact it is, great view of the ball game, if there was one."

"I have a feeling we won't be watching."

"No, they'll be watching us."

"Lighting guys won't save you there."

"No, that's your job."

"I'll find the blinds."

"Keep the lights on though."

"Always the dramatic."

"Well I am a Diva."

As the tour crew removes the stage from the stadium, and the lights are dim, you can just see a set of windows up above closing its blinds and putting its lights on. The shadow show of them having sex was like watching on a big screen, but with the seats too far away.

THE END

AFTERWORD

I hope you enjoyed reading this book. Absolutely none of the situations which happen in this romantic comedy have ever occurred in my life. Well, not exactly as written, some hints of life before high school, I really did attend a party where Stairway to Heaven played non-stop, either by LP on a turntable or by piano… no tapes or CDs back then circa 1980.

I do play an online scrabble-type game with a high school friend that was someone's crush. I've never run out of gasoline with a rental car, I've busted engines with three of my own, and I've certainly never been a pop diva strip teasing for anyone that smelled bad.

If you're reading this first, you're cheating, stop now and go to the beginning! I think I covered all the basics, two women, one guy conflict, and he wins her heart in the end.

ACKNOWLEDGEMENTS

I would greatly like to thank Cheyenne for bringing another person's opinion to my first draft. She praised it as being the next "Notebook" and simply couldn't put it down. Paul Tracy who has a cameo in the book gave me permission on Twitter to include him. By the time you read this he should have an Indy Car ride because he deserves it.

The cover image of my book was done by Brianna Klint copyright 2009. She has her own artwork website Briezy's Drawings.

I can only hope you enjoyed reading this story about a struggling stand-up comedian and the pop diva girlfriend of his dreams.

ABOUT THE AUTHOR

As you know if you've read every page in this book, I've written a variety of books, in style and description. Perhaps because I was born a Gemini, five days later than my expected arrival of 6/6/66, perhaps I needed to be less evil.

I live in a town where pretty much noone can drive properly, has far too many grocery stores, and politicians with too many hands in coffers where they shouldn't be.

My day job is basically a one hour plus, each way commute from hell, with some slightly less stressful ridiculous construction deadlines for that firm with the big green U logo. It seems when you're good at something, not only are you expected to do it quickly, but you must sit patiently while every job that needs to be done gets handed to you with five minutes left in the day, and that's exactly when your computer decides its had enough and crashes on you.

Do I resemble any of the main characters? Take a wild guess.